Rosie

This series is for my riding friend Shelley,
who cares about all animals.

Visit the Animal Magic website:
www.animalmagicrescue.net

STRIPES PUBLISHING
An imprint of Magi Publications
1 The Coda Centre, 189 Munster Road, London SW6 6AW

A paperback original
First published in Great Britain in 2009

ISBN: 978-1-84715-076-9

A CIP catalogue record for this book is available from the British Library.

Printed and bound in the UK.

2 4 6 8 10 9 7 5 3

Rosie

Tina Nolan
Illustrated by Sharon Rentta

stripes

 # ANIMAL MAGIC

Meet the animals

Visit our website at
www.animalmagicrescue.net

Working our
magic to match
the perfect pet
with the perfect
owner!

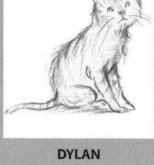

DYLAN

Meet Dylan. He's young
and very affectionate,
waiting patiently for that
special person to give
him the love he needs.

BOSWELL

Silky and soft, and
very hard to say no to,
lovely Boswell is neutered
and house-trained too!

JERRY

A gorgeous short-haired
collie-cross who loves to
play. Lively Jerry needs
lots of walks!

RESCUE CENTRE
in need of a home!

BUTCH

There's a lot of bull mastiff in Butch, but we can't say exactly how old he is or where he came from. Will need lots of TLC.

LOTTIE

A little sweetie who's been living rough on an allotment. She's looking forward to finding a loving new owner.

TOFFEE AND FUDGE

This gorgeous pair are friendly and like being picked up. Can you give them a home together?

FREDDIE

Freddie the terrier is adorably soft and cuddly and will follow you wherever you go!

Chapter One

"Bye, Mum! Bye, Dad!" Eva Harrison stood outside Passport Control, waving as her parents disappeared into the Departure Lounge.

"Don't forget – take lots of pictures of you swimming with dolphins!" Eva's brother, Karl, called after them.

"Watch out for alligators!" Eva's voice was drowned out by the din of an airport announcement.

Karl and Eva's grandfather, Jimmy

Harrison, waited until Heidi and Mark were out of sight, then took over. "Come on, Eva, time to go." He led her and Karl through the check-in hall and out to the car park. "Don't worry about them," he smiled. "They're going to have a fantastic time in Florida. And this holiday is your dad's surprise late Christmas present to your mum, so they're bound to have fun."

Eva nodded as she climbed into the Land Rover. "I know, Grandad. I'm really glad they've gone on holiday, but I'm still going to miss them."

"Well, we'll be so busy at Animal Magic that you won't have *time* to miss them," Karl warned. "We won't have a spare second to think about them sunning themselves on a beach with palm trees, looking out at a blue sea, snorkelling, swimming with dolphins..."

"Stop, you're making me jealous!" Eva held her hands over her ears. It was Friday – New Year's Eve – and the snow that had fallen over Christmas had long since melted. Now England was grey and damp, the clouds were heavy and the days short. Eva sighed, then stared out of the window at the wet city streets.

"Cheer up, Eva," Jimmy said, grinning.

"I happen to know that, besides arranging emergency vet cover while they're away, your mum and dad have lined up a nice surprise for you and Karl later today."

Karl leaned forward from the back seat. "What kind of surprise?"

"If I told you now, it wouldn't be a surprise, would it?" their grandad laughed.

"Tell us anyway," Eva begged. She was thinking that it might be a trip to the cinema or a visit to their favourite pizza restaurant.

"No, I'm sworn to secrecy!" Leaving the city behind, Jimmy followed a dual carriageway, then took the exit marked Okeham. Pretty soon they were driving through farmland and heading for home.

"Hey, Karl, I'm glad you're back. I was hoping you'd feed the cats," Jen said the minute he walked into Reception at Animal Magic. Jen, the centre's veterinary assistant, was standing in for Mark and Heidi while they were on holiday, and she seemed run off her feet already.

"No problem," Karl said, hurrying down the corridor to the storeroom.

"And Eva, could you come into the surgery and help me with Dylan?"

Eva waved goodbye to her grandad, then followed Jen into the surgery where she saw a pet carrier on the examination table. Inside the carrier was a sad-looking ginger cat, half covered by a dirty fleece blanket.

"Dylan's owner dropped him off half an hour ago," Jen explained. She put on a pair of surgical gloves and dumped the blanket in the bin before lifting the cat out of the carrier and placing him carefully on the scrubbed, shiny table. "She wasn't best pleased with you, was she, poor thing?"

Eva noticed that the little cat looked miserable. "Why, what did he do?"

"It's not something he did, actually." Carefully, Jen opened Dylan's mouth and peered inside, then examined his eyes. "He's covered in fleas, poor chap, and his owner is complaining that she's developed a skin condition called flea allergy dermatitis."

"So she's left him with us?" Eva checked. She was feeling more and more sorry for the shivering cat.

Jen nodded. "She said there was no chance of having him back, so I promised we'd rehome him once we've dealt with the fleas."

"How come the owner didn't treat them herself?"

"I haven't a clue," Jen answered. "It doesn't look as if she even bothered to wash his bedding, judging by the state of that blanket. Uh-oh, Eva, I wouldn't stroke Dylan if I were you – not yet."

Eva stepped back. "We'll take a photo and Karl can put him on the website straight away," she decided. "What Dylan needs is someone who gives him regular flea treatments, plus lots of cuddles!"

"Exactly," Jen agreed. She returned the patient to the carrier and prepared to carry him into the quarantine section of the cattery. "I did have one good piece of news while you were at the airport."

Eva followed her down the corridor. "What is it?"

"Some people saw Jerry on the website – they want to come in and take a proper look at him."

Jerry was a gorgeous short-haired collie-cross who had been in the Animal Magic kennels since long before Christmas. Now it seemed his luck was in. "Did they sound nice?" Eva asked.

"Yes, very," Jen replied, stepping aside to let Karl hurry ahead to the cattery with two dishes of cat food. "Karl, I was telling Eva – we've got someone interested in adopting Jerry."

"Cool!" Karl had a soft spot for the collie-cross, who was playful and full of energy. "When are they coming in?"

"Tomorrow's Saturday, isn't it? So, tomorrow at two o'clock. They're called Jane and Rob Goodall. I wrote the appointment in the diary."

"OK. But right now we have to make sure we feed Dylan up," Eva told Karl as Jen put the new arrival in isolation at the end of the row of cats all needing good homes. She paused by Lottie the allotment cat's cage and peered in. "You're looking good," she murmured, smiling as Lottie purred, then tucked in to her meal. Then Eva ran after Jen, who had gone on into the small animals' unit.

"Meet another new arrival." Jen lifted a grey and white rabbit out of a cage.

"He's cute!" Eva stroked the silky fur. "What's his name?"

"This is Boswell. He's an unwanted Christmas present."

"Aah – you're lovely!" Eva assured him as she took him from Jen. She liked the way he twitched his ears and wrinkled his nose at the same time. "Don't worry – someone will snap you up and give you a great new home."

"After we've neutered you and given you a thorough health check," Jen added. "By the way, I haven't had time to ask – did your mum and dad get off safely?"

Eva cuddled Boswell and nodded. "They're in the air right now, lucky things."

Jen stroked the rabbit, then helped Eva to put him back in his cage. Then they hurried back into Reception.

"What I don't get's why they left you all by yourself." Eva had been puzzled by this. It wasn't like her mum to push lots of responsibility on to her assistant.

"I'm not by myself – I've got you and Karl." Looking mysterious, Jen began to tidy some paperwork on the desk. "And you're still on your school holidays so I'm sure we'll cope very well."

Eva nodded. If every day was as busy as today, she wasn't sure they would. But she didn't say anything to Jen. Instead she went to stick some new notices on the board by the window. "Jen, is it OK if I go to the house and check on Holly?" she asked when she'd finished.

"Sure. I'm surprised you've lasted this long!" Jen smiled as Eva darted off.

Holly was the adorable new addition to the Harrison family – a black and white

Border collie puppy who'd come to them on Christmas Eve. In one week she'd made herself completely at home in the kitchen of the old farmhouse. She had her own bed by the side of the fire, her favourite spot under the table and a cheeky habit of jumping up into the lap of whoever came in for coffee.

"Holly, where are you?" Eva cried as she ran into the kitchen.

"She's in here," Karl called from the sitting room. He'd finished feeding the cats and beaten Eva to it.

Eva hurried into the hallway. "Hey, Holly, it's me!"

Like a shot the pup scrambled to meet her, jumping up and yelping with joy.

"Down, Holly!" Eva ordered, trying not to burst into delighted laughter.

The excited puppy jumped up again.

Then she squirmed on the floor, leaving a small puddle on the tiles.

"Uh-oh, the dreaded excitement wee!" Grinning, Eva went back into the kitchen for the mop. Holly saw it and pounced. "No, Holly. This is a mop, not something to play with!" She was still dealing with the puddle when Karl appeared.

"Hey, Eva, come in here," he said with a mysterious smile.

"What's the big secret?" Eva propped the mop against the wall and went into the sitting room – to find Joel standing there.

"Hello, Eva."

"Joel!" She ran to hug the young veterinary assistant who had left Animal Magic a few months earlier to go and work in Russia. "Why? I mean, what are…?" Eva paused mid-sentence. "…Hey, are *you* our surprise?"

Joel gave her a wide grin. "Yes! I'm home for the New Year."

"Wow!" Eva was speechless. She'd missed seeing Joel's kind, smiling face around the place and his scruffy Beetle car parked out in the yard. "Happy New Year! Cool surprise!"

"It gets better," Karl promised, scooping Holly up as she ran between his legs. "Tell her, Joel."

"I'm here for a couple of weeks, and I told Heidi that rather than just sitting around twiddling my thumbs, I'd help out here."

"At Animal Magic?" Eva gasped.

"Where else?" Joel grinned. "In fact, I'm off to the surgery to help Jen."

"Right now?" Eva gasped.

"Right this very minute." Joel laughed as he walked out of the house and across the yard.

Chapter Two

"Happy New Year!" Annie Brooks greeted Eva from Rosie's stable.

It was Saturday and Eva had got up early to bring Annie the surprise news about Joel.

"Yeah, Happy New Year!" she gasped now, grinning at Annie and seizing a mucking-out fork. "It definitely is a happy, Happy New Year!"

"Why, what's happened?" Annie asked, as Rosie, the cheeky Shetland pony, gave her a nudge in the back, then barged past to stick her shaggy head over the door.

"Hi, Rosie." Eva grinned. She stroked the pony's nose. "Joel's only come back to help out at Animal Magic – that's all!"

"Hey, cool! How long's he staying?"

The two girls chatted as Eva got stuck in to mucking out Guinevere and Merlin's stable. "Until Mum and Dad get back. Jen says she's glad of the help, and of course Joel already knows everything about the rescue centre. Hey, are you going to keep the horses in today or turn them out into the field?"

Annie glanced up at the blue sky. "Mum said to let them out."

"It's cold," Eva warned. "There's ice on all the paths."

"Maybe we'll just leave them out for the morning, then bring them in again."

Annie went to the tack room to fetch the horses' rugs while Eva forked muck into a wheelbarrow.

"It's so cool – Joel's been telling us about working in Russia. He loves it."

"Here's Merlin's rug," Annie interrupted. "Stand still, Rosie, while I put yours on."

Quickly, Eva slid the horse rug over young Merlin's back and buckled the straps. She smiled to herself as she heard the scuffle next door.

"Stand still, Rosie. I can't do the straps if you dance around like that. That's better. No, I haven't got any treats in my pocket – stop that, you naughty thing!"

By the time Annie had finished with Rosie, Eva had rugged Guinevere and let her and Merlin out into the frosty field.

The grey mare and her foal trotted off down the slope. They'd spotted Karl on the riverside path and gone to say hello.

"Hi, Karl!" Eva waved and ran to join them. "What are you up to?"

"I'm taking Jerry for a walk before the Goodalls come to see him," he explained. "And I brought Holly along too."

"Aah!" Leaning over the fence, Eva laughed to see little Holly on the end of the lead. The puppy was snuffling in the long grass. Then she lifted her head to shake off the white frost from the tip of her black nose.

"Watch out, here comes Rosie," Karl warned.

At last Annie had got Rosie's rug on, and now the sturdy Shetland was frisking down the slope.

"Wait for me!" Annie called, zipping up her thick jacket and coming to join Eva and Karl.

"How's Rosie settling in?" Karl asked Annie. It was less than two weeks since Rosie had moved in to the Brookses' new stables. Before that the pony had stayed next door at Animal Magic, waiting for someone to adopt her.

"Good," Annie reported. "She still gets on well with Gwinnie and Merlin."

"Who's the boss out of the three of them?" Karl asked. He let Jerry off the lead to run along the riverside path.

"Rosie!" Annie answered quickly. "She's the smallest, but she definitely orders the other two around."

As if to prove it, Rosie began to nudge and push at Merlin as if she was rounding him up and herding him back up the hill.

Eva and Karl laughed. "We miss her," Eva said.

"Mum says she's a little character." Annie smiled. "Hey, what's she up to now?"

Rosie had suddenly broken away from Merlin and was making a beeline for the fence which separated the Brookses' field from the yard at Animal Magic. She covered the ground as fast as her little legs would carry her.

"Rosie, stop!" Eva yelled. She chased after the pony, trying to head her off before she reached the boundary.

But Rosie wouldn't listen. She charged straight at the high fence.

"Uh-oh, she's going to jump!" Karl cringed and closed his eyes. "I can't look."

"She's too small, she'll never make it," Annie wailed.

Eva sprinted across the field and got to the fence seconds before Rosie. She stood in the pony's path, waving both arms above her head, warning her away.

At the last second, Rosie put on the brakes and slid to a stop along the frosty ground, digging up the turf just inches from the high fence.

"No way was that a good idea!" Eva told her sternly. "If you want to come and visit us, you have to be sensible and let Annie lead you through the gate."

Rosie snickered then trotted up to Eva.

"OK, so now you're sorry." Eva laughed, relenting and letting cheeky Rosie push her nose against her hand. "But just remember – this is your home now. So no more crazy ideas about getting back to Animal Magic!"

Eva spent the afternoon in the kennels. She bathed a grey, short-coated cross-breed with a lot of bull mastiff in him. The stray had arrived at lunchtime, covered in mud and lame in his front foot. A woman driving her car on the main road into the city had seen him limping along the grass verge. Since he wasn't wearing a collar, the woman had decided to bring him into the rescue centre.

"If only people would microchip their

pets," Jen sighed, watching Eva set about cleaning the dog up. "We'll hold him for a while in case the owner comes looking, but my guess is he'll end up on our website."

Eva sponged the dog down, then rubbed him dry. "Don't worry – I'm going to choose a name for you... Let's call you Butch! And we'll find you a lovely, kind new owner," she promised.

Further down the row of kennels, Karl was busy sprucing up Jerry, ready for his appointment with the Goodalls. "You're looking smart," he murmured.

Just then, Joel popped his head around the door. "Eva, do you mind giving me a hand with two new arrivals?"

"No problem." Giving Butch one last rub, she put him safely back in his kennel and dashed to Reception.

"Oh, and Karl, the Goodalls are here,"

Joel added. "Bring Jerry through."

"It's your big moment," Karl told Jerry, putting him on the lead and following Eva and Joel out of the kennels.

"Two more strays." Joel showed Eva the small cage on top of the reception desk. "Brought in by Pete Knight from Main Street. He found them hiding in his garden shed, searching for a bit of warmth."

Curious, Eva peered into the cage to see two guinea pigs – one toffee coloured, one brown and white. They were huddled in a corner, scrabbling at the floor of the cage with their pink front feet.

"Jen examined them and says they're both males. Would you like to choose names?" Joel asked Eva.

"Hmm... How about Toffee and Fudge?" She grinned as the names popped into her head.

"Nice one. Toffee and Fudge it is. I'm sure they'll be snapped up the minute you put them on the website."

Eva nodded, and then she stepped aside to let Jerry make his big entrance with Karl. There was a middle-aged man and a woman sitting in the waiting area, looking nervous but eager.

"This is Jerry," Karl told the couple. "Sit, Jerry!"

The obedient dog instantly followed his command.

"He's sweet," Mrs Goodall said. "See his eyes – they look intelligent."

"He's quite lively when you take him out for a walk," Karl warned her.

"Will he come back when you call him?" Mr Goodall asked.

Karl nodded. "Would you like to come for a walk and see him in action?"

"Great idea," Mr Goodall agreed. "We don't want to adopt him and then find out that he's too much for us to handle."

So, while Karl took Jerry and the Goodalls for a walk by the river, Eva helped Joel with Toffee and Fudge. "I'll take their photo for the website," she decided. "Joel, can you hold them, one in each hand? Look this way, you two. That's it – smile!"

"You know how to upload the picture yourself, don't you?" Joel asked, taking a quick look at the result.

"Yes. Shall I do it now?"

"Feel free," Joel said, hurrying on to his next job.

So Eva sat at the computer. She put the cute picture on to the Animal Magic website, then began to type. "Toffee and Fudge." She stopped to compose the next sentence, then began again. "Friendly and like to be picked up." *Hmm, I should mention how gorgeous and cuddly they are,* she thought.

Before she could add anything else, the phone rang and Eva picked it up. "Hello, this is Animal Magic."

"Hello, Animal Magic, this is Mark Harrison!"

"Dad!" Eva gasped. "Where are you?"

"In Miami Beach, in the best hotel in the world," he said. "I'm sitting on a balcony overlooking the sea. It's magic."

"Have you seen any dolphins?" Eva asked.

"Not yet. How are you, Eva? How's Karl? Is he there?"

"No. He's out with Jerry. We think we've found him a home."

"Good, fingers crossed. Did you like our surprise?"

"You mean Joel? So cool!" Eva answered happily, smiling as Joel himself came across to take the phone.

"Listen, Mark, you're not allowed to ask any questions about work," he warned. "This is your holiday, remember."

Seeing Karl come back into the yard with Jerry and the Goodalls, Eva ran to open the door.

Mrs Goodall led Jerry in on the lead. "Good boy, Jerry. Sit!"

He sat by her side, staring up at her with his big, brown eyes.

"Well?" Eva asked.

"He's wonderful!" Mrs Goodall sighed. "I can picture us taking him for walks in the woods behind our house, throwing a stick and getting him to fetch it."

"In other words, we'll take him," her husband said with a smile.

Jerry seemed to understand. He gave a yelp of pleasure, stood up and wagged his tail to a bright new future with Mr and Mrs Goodall.

Chapter Three

That night Eva slept soundly and woke early, well before she thought Karl or Jen would be up. She put on her dressing gown and crept downstairs into the kitchen to spend one-on-one time with Holly.

"Hi!" she whispered.

The puppy was thrilled to see her. She leaped from her basket and ran across the kitchen floor towards Eva. Eva picked her up and let her snuggle into her arms.

"Sshh! Don't wake the others," she whispered, tiptoeing through into the sitting room.

"No need to whisper," Karl grinned. "I'm already awake!"

Awake and watching TV, stretched out on the sofa with a bowl of cereal resting on his chest. Eva stared in disbelief.

"No need to look like that. I've been up ages. I've already taken Holly on her morning walk."

In the background, the music for the start of the Tina O'Neill show began and the chat show host appeared on-screen. She ran through the items on the morning programme – an interview with a big movie director, and the chance to enter an exciting competition, but before that an item on a series of children's pony books written by a famous actress.

"Boring!" Karl sighed. He was about to switch channels when Eva stopped him.

"Leave it on. I want to see the bit about the pony books."

"I can't stand chat shows," Karl said. But he gave way to Eva, and they watched the host introduce the celeb at home in her converted farm.

Eva sat cross-legged in front of the TV with Holly in her lap. "Look at the ponies, Holly!"

"It's no secret that I love horses," Tina's voice went on, while the camera panned over a green field dotted with beautiful thoroughbreds. "But I still wonder what persuaded top actress Venus Hall to break into the world of pony books?"

The camera settled on a tall, slim figure dressed in jodhpurs and long black boots. "Ever since I was a little girl I dreamed of having my own pony," Venus replied.

"Blah, blah!" Karl snorted.

"So the books are a way of making your childhood dream come true?" Tina asked.

"Exactly." Venus nodded.

"Holly, sit!" Eva said as the puppy leaped off her lap and barked at the TV screen. She leaned forward to pick her up, but Holly darted round the back of the TV. "Mind the wires!" Eva cried. "Karl, turn the TV off, quick, in case Holly gets an electric shock!"

There was a scuffle behind the TV before Eva emerged triumphant. "I'll take Holly back into the kitchen – it's safer there," she decided.

"Good, now I can switch channels," Karl grunted.

Back in the kitchen, the phone was ringing. It was Annie, wanting to know if Eva would like to ride Guinevere.

"When?" Eva asked.

"Now," Annie told her.

"OK, I'll check with Jen."

Luckily, Jen had just come downstairs in her dressing gown. Quickly, Eva asked permission, then spoke into the phone again. "Give me five minutes to get dressed," she gabbled, "and I'll be right there!"

Out in the Brookses' field, Eva found that her friend had already saddled Guinevere, but was struggling with the bridle.

"Gwinnie keeps on raising her head so I can't reach her mouth," she complained.

In the stable next door, Rosie gave a shrill neigh and a hefty kick at the door.

"Hi, Rosie!" Eva replied cheerfully. She took the bridle from Annie and slipped the reins over Gwinnie's head. "This should do the trick," she promised.

Sure enough, the horse felt the reins hanging loose around her neck and saw Eva waiting patiently with the bit in her hand. Obediently, she lowered her head and waited for Eva to slip the bit between her teeth.

Annie nodded. "Cool. Here's the hard hat. You have first turn," she offered.

Eva put on the hat while Annie opened

the stable door and stood back.

Another kick at her door told them Rosie wanted to come too.

"Stay here, Rosie. We won't be long," Annie told the Shetland, giving her a quick stroke.

"How long has she been kicking the door?" Eva asked, as she put her feet in the stirrups, and set off slowly down the field.

"For a couple of days. Listen, Mum wants us to stay in the field," Annie told Eva. "She says not to go above a trot."

So Eva rode steadily, letting Gwinnie take her time. Back at the stable, naughty Rosie was still kicking and banging, and the back door to Annie's house had opened.

"Uh-oh, I bet Mum's mad," Annie muttered, leaving Eva to ride and jogging

back up the hill. But before she reached the stable, Rosie had landed an extra-hard kick and forced the bolt. The stable door flew open and the little pony barged out in a bid for freedom.

"No, go back!" Annie yelled.

By now Linda Brooks had come out into her garden and started to run down the path towards the field.

Taking no notice of Annie, Rosie tried the same trick as the day before. She galloped towards the fence, looking for all the world as if she was going to clear it and land in the yard at Animal Magic.

"Oh no!" Annie wailed.

Her mum sprinted down the path.

"Come on, Gwinnie, trot on!" Eva cried, urging the horse to catch up with Rosie. Guinevere's long legs quickly covered the ground. "Oh no you don't!" Eva shouted, getting into position to cut Rosie off again. Just in time, she got to the right spot and stood her ground.

Once more, the pony threatened to jump and stopped at the last second. She lowered her head so that her shaggy brown mane covered her eyes, then she glanced up cheekily at Eva.

"It's not funny!" Eva sighed, signalling to

Annie that everything was OK.

Annie waved back, then ran to tell her mum.

But it was her dad who greeted her from the garden.

"Where's Mum?" Annie asked. The last she'd known, her mum had been sprinting down the path to see what had caused the rumpus in the field.

"Your mum's had a fall," Jason Brooks explained over the garden fence. "She slipped on the ice."

"Mum, are you all right?" Annie gasped, spotting Linda leaning heavily against a low garden wall.

Her dad shook his head. "She'll be OK, but I'm going to drive her to hospital to have her leg X-rayed. It'll be best if you stay with Eva."

"Can't I come?" Annie begged.

But her
dad told
her she had
to stay.
"I'll call
you as soon as
we have any news,"
he promised, rushing off to help Linda
into the car.

By the time Eva had ridden up and slid
out of the saddle, Annie was in tears.

"It's all Rosie's fault!" she cried. "Mum's
had an accident."

It took a while for Eva to understand,
but when she did, she quickly unsaddled
Gwinnie and put her in the stable. In the
background she heard the sound of Jason
Brooks's car driving out on to Main Street.
"Wait here while I get Rosie back into her
stable," she told Annie.

Soon all the horses were inside and Eva took Annie back to her house. She led her into the kitchen where Jen was cooking bacon. "Linda's had an accident," she explained. "Rosie was trying to escape again. Linda tried to stop her and she slipped on some ice. I'm not sure, but I think Rosie's limping too."

Jen quickly took control. "Karl, you can finish making your bacon sandwich, can't you? I'm going to pop next door and take a look at Rosie. Eva, you stay here to keep Annie company."

It seemed like ages before Jen returned, but at last the kitchen door opened and she appeared.

"You're right, Eva. Rosie's lame," she confirmed. "Her right knee is swollen. Did she knock it against something?"

"Against the door," Eva told her, nodding.

"Poor Rosie – she kicked it so hard she forced it open."

"In that case, I'll give her a painkiller and something to help bring down the swelling, and then she'll need box-rest. With luck she won't have done any real damage."

Relieved, Eva turned to Annie. "Let's hope we get some good news about your mum, too," she murmured.

But when the phone went an hour later and Jason spoke to Annie, the news was bad. "They've just X-rayed your mum's leg and found she's broken it in two places," he told her, sounding upset.

Shocked, Annie handed the phone to Eva.

"Tell Annie not to worry," Jason Brooks insisted. "Her mum will be fine. The doctor will put her leg in a plaster cast and she'll be on crutches for a couple of months. But the leg will get better, tell her."

"I will," Eva promised.

"And say we'll be home by lunchtime." Mr Brooks concluded. "Tell her everything is going to be fine."

Chapter Four

Gradually, the shock of Linda's accident wore off.

"It could have been worse," Jen told Annie. "And I'm sure the hospital is taking good care of your mum."

"It could happen to anyone," Karl said. "The Accident and Emergency department must be full of people who've slipped on the ice in weather like this."

"Does it hurt a lot when you break your leg?" Annie asked anxiously.

"Only until the doctors give you a painkiller," Jen explained. "A bit like the medicine I gave Rosie."

Talking things over, they waited patiently for Jason to bring Linda home. Then, as soon as Annie heard their car, she said a hurried goodbye and ran to meet them.

A few minutes later, Joel's Beetle appeared in the yard and Eva rushed out to tell him what had happened.

"Whoa!" Joel cried after Eva's garbled account. "Who broke their leg – Rosie or Linda?"

"Linda. But Rosie's lame, too. I don't know what got into her, charging the fence like that."

"Twice!" Karl added. He'd followed Eva out of the house with Holly.

"She's usually so good," Eva insisted. "But she seemed to think that if she jumped the fence she could get back to Animal Magic."

"Hmm. I wonder why." Joel agreed that it was a mystery. "But listen, you two, we've got work to do. Dogs and cats to feed, small animal cages to clean out, a website to update..."

Eva was glad to be busy. Sunday afternoon was filled with chores, and when they'd finally finished at the rescue centre, Eva and Joel paid a visit to Rosie in her stable. It was already growing dark and there was no sign of Annie, Linda or Jason.

"We'll check the swelling on Rosie's leg without bothering the Brookses," Joel told Eva. "They probably want a quiet evening to get over the shock of the accident."

So they went into the stable to find Rosie standing in a corner looking sorry for herself. She was keeping the weight off her injured leg and blowing softly through her nose.

"There!" Eva said gently. She stroked Rosie's neck while Joel ran his hand over the swollen knee.

"It feels warm," he reported. "The joint is inflamed, but she's not too uncomfortable when I touch it."

"There, Rosie," Eva breathed. "You hear that? You're going to be fine."

"I'll give her a thorough examination while I'm here," Joel decided. He looked for the light switch outside the stable door.

"Hello there, Joel." Jason Brooks appeared round the side of the stables. "I was in the garden throwing grit on the path. I heard noises."

"Hi, Mr Brooks," Eva broke in. "Joel and Jen both think that Rosie's injury isn't too bad. She'll just need box-rest for a few days." She noticed that Annie's dad seemed to be frowning in the sudden glare of electric light.

"And how's Linda?" Joel asked.

Jason sighed. "She's in bed. Her leg's in

plaster up to the hip and the painkiller really seems to have knocked her sideways. I'm hoping she'll get a good night's sleep."

"Let's hope so." Joel realized how tired Jason must be. "Is it OK for me to top up Rosie with another dose of painkiller in her evening feed?"

"Yes, go ahead." Jason watched Joel mix the sachet into Rosie's feed bucket. "Linda and I were talking on the drive back from hospital. I said that I thought perhaps she'd taken on too much. Three horses need a lot of looking after."

Instinctively, Eva put her arm around Rosie's neck.

"Give Rosie a chance to settle in," Joel suggested. "She won't be any trouble in the long run."

"I'm not so sure," Jason argued.

"Apparently she spent the whole of yesterday evening trying to kick her door down, and she was at it again early this morning. That's how Linda fell – she was hurrying out to see what the fuss was about."

"Sshh!" Eva told Rosie as the pony raised her head and gave a shrill neigh.

There was a long pause before Jason spoke again. "Linda and I are both surprised by what a handful Rosie can be."

"She's not usually..." Eva began to protest, but Joel gave her a warning glance.

"I'm sorry you feel that way, Jason. But you need to give it time."

Jason Brooks seemed too upset to take any notice of Joel's reasoning. "There's not much point now that this has happened," he argued. "Linda's leg is in plaster and it's going to be impossible for her to look after *three* horses."

"Does Linda agree?" Joel asked.

No! Eva prayed she wasn't hearing this. She wanted to wind back time to before the accident, then play it through again, this time with a happy ending for Rosie.

"She sees the sense of what I'm saying,"

Jason replied. "And we agree that Rosie doesn't seem to have settled in as well as we'd hoped."

"I see," Joel said calmly. He stood back to watch Rosie feed. "I think we understand what you're telling us, don't we, Eva?"

Eva bit her lip. *Please, Mr Brooks, don't do this!* she thought.

Jason sighed. "I'm sorry, but Rosie's too much for us to handle. So I'm afraid we'll be sending her back to Animal Magic – the sooner the better."

Chapter Five

Both Annie and Eva were in tears over Rosie.

"Please persuade your dad to change his mind!" Eva begged. She'd run into the Brookses' house after Jason had broken the news and found Annie sobbing in her bedroom. "Tell him you have to keep Rosie!"

"I've tried," Annie cried. She sat cross-legged on her bed, covering her face with her hands. "Honestly, Eva – he won't listen."

"But your mum's accident wasn't Rosie's fault. It was the ice on the path that made her slip."

"I know!" Annie cried even harder. "Oh Eva, this is all my fault. I shouldn't have blamed Rosie for Mum's accident. I only did it because I was so upset."

"No, it isn't your fault either," Eva insisted. "But listen, when your dad has calmed down, maybe you can talk to him again. Tell him I'll come twice a day to help with the mucking out. We can do it between us."

Just then, Jason Brooks passed Annie's bedroom door. "I know you mean well," he told Eva, "but even before Linda had her accident, we were beginning to think that Rosie wasn't happy here. Now it seems that something – fate, or whatever you like to call it – is definitely telling us

that we're not the right owners for her."
He shook his head sadly, then walked on.

Annie sobbed quietly. "Dad means it,
Eva. He won't change his mind."

Eva wiped her cheeks and sighed. "OK,
I'll tell Karl."

"Tell him what?" Annie sniffed.

"To put Rosie's details back on the
Animal Magic website. Starting tomorrow,
we'll look for another home for her."

The silence after she spoke hung heavy in the air. They both thought of Rosie with her shaggy mane and mischievous eyes, her jaunty trot and cheeky habit of snuffling at your pocket for an apple or a carrot.

"I'm so sorry!" Annie said at last.

Eva nodded. "Me too," she said as she left the room.

"We're still friends, aren't we?"

"Of course," Eva assured her sadly. "I'll see you, Annie. Bye."

"The thing that gets me", Eva told Karl as she sat beside him in Reception on Monday morning, "is that Mr Brooks thinks Rosie's a problem, and she's not!"

"Rosie the problem pony," Karl muttered. He looked through old files for her details, ready to put them back on the site.

"Rosie the *perfect* pony!" Eva insisted. "Make her sound good, Karl. Tell everybody how cute she is."

"Hold it, you two." Jen came and looked over their shoulders. "Don't say anything that isn't true. We can't afford to mislead anyone."

"But what did she do wrong?" Eva refused to believe anything bad about the gorgeous Rosie.

"Nearly kicked the stable door down for a start," Jen pointed out. "And she tried to escape at least twice, didn't she? I'm not being unkind, Eva, but you must admit she didn't settle in well at the Brookses'."

"She did at first," Eva muttered. "Everything was OK until this weekend."

"Hmm, strange that." Though Joel was busy admitting a new puppy, he joined in the conversation. "I wonder what went wrong all of a sudden. Anyway, Eva, let Karl get on with the website entry. Why don't you come and help me with Freddie?"

Eva followed him into an examination room where he took a puppy out of a pet carrier and placed him on the table. "Here's another unwanted Christmas present," he explained. "But not the sort you can take back to the shop and get a refund on."

Eva tutted. "And he's gorgeous. Aren't you beautiful, Freddie?" She stroked the long-haired, cream-coloured puppy – a terrier type with big, pointed ears and a short tail.

Joel smiled. "He seems healthy, so I'll get him chipped and vaccinated; then we can take him into the kennels, settle him down and give him a drink."

"I'll fill a water bowl," Eva offered, glad to have her mind taken off Rosie. But as she made her way towards the kennels, she saw her grandad drive into the yard and she did a rapid detour. "Hi, Grandad. Guess who we've got back in our stables!"

"Hello, Eva. I've got no idea." Jimmy Harrison grinned as he climbed out of his car. "But I'm sure I'm about to find out!"

"Rosie!" Eva declared. "Joel brought her back from the Brookses' place early this morning – before Annie was up so she didn't get too upset having to see Rosie leave. She's in here. Come and look."

Jimmy followed Eva into the clean, airy stables. They found Rosie in the nearest stall, her head poking over the door.

"Tell me honestly, Grandad, does Rosie look like a problem pony to you?"

Newly brushed, with her mane combed and her lively eyes shining, the little Shetland looked picture-book perfect.

Jimmy smiled. "No, she doesn't. But it's not what I think that counts. Now, Eva, come inside the house and share these lovely warm croissants with me. I bought them specially at the supermarket."

"Yum!" If one thing could drag Eva away from the animals, it was food. The croissants smelt good as she put them on a plate and her grandfather made himself coffee. In the background the TV was on, showing Tina O'Neill interviewing another of her celebrity guests.

"Chat-chat-chitter-chat," Jimmy groaned, turning the TV off.

But Eva didn't hear him. She sat with her half-eaten croissant raised to her lips.

"What's wrong?" her grandad asked.

"What? Erm, nothing. Grandad, do you mind if I go now? Joel asked me to help with Freddie the terrier. Bye!"

"No, I don't mind." Jimmy grinned as Eva sprinted off across the yard. Then he shook his head. "Funny, that. She doesn't usually turn her nose up at warm croissants..."

"OK, everyone, I'm going now." Joel popped his head around the kitchen door. It had been a busy day as usual, and Jen was cooking the evening meal of pasta with tomato sauce.

"Stay to eat," Jen invited. "There's plenty of food."

Joel nodded. "If you're sure."

"Sure!" Jen insisted.

Eva set an extra place at the table. She hummed a tune she'd been repeating all day as she went about her business in the kennels and the cattery, cleaning out the small animal cages and taking care of Rosie.

"There was one thing I wanted to do before I left," Joel remembered suddenly. "I was going to check Rosie, so I'll quickly do it now."

"I'll come!" Eva volunteered in a flash.

"Karl's still in the surgery. Tell him supper will be ready in ten minutes," Jen called after them.

"How's Rosie's leg?" Eva asked Joel as they hurried towards the stable.

Rosie whinnied a greeting. Her shaggy mane had fallen back over her eyes since Eva's morning grooming session.

"The swelling's going down nicely," Joel reported. He picked up the pony's feet to examine them closely. "No – nothing to worry about there."

"What are you looking for?" Eva asked, stroking Rosie's neck.

Joel frowned. "I'm not sure. Something – anything that would make Rosie kick her door and take off across the field."

Eva nodded. "Yes, there must be a reason," she agreed. "Rosie isn't normally like that."

"And it wasn't anything to do with the way Linda and Annie treated her?"

"No." Eva couldn't fault her neighbours. "They mucked her out properly, brushed her every day, gave her plenty of food and water."

"So why were you unhappy?" Joel asked quietly as he ran his hand along the pony's broad back.

Rosie shifted sideways, away from Joel and Eva.

"Hmm. OK, we'll leave you in peace," Joel decided. "Come on, Eva, close the door behind you. We'd better not keep Jen waiting."

The warm kitchen was full of delicious smells. Holly dozed on her bed in the corner.

"Did you remember to tell Karl food was ready?" Jen asked.

"Oops! I'll go and get him," Eva said.

"No need!" Karl announced, flinging open the door. He waved a sheet of paper under Eva's nose. "Look what I found!"

Eva gasped as she tried to grab the paper from him. "You snoop!"

"Honestly, Eva – only you could think up something as crazy as this!"

"Karl, leave Eva alone," Jen told him.

He laid the paper flat on the table. "I knew from your face that you were up to something," he went on. "You've been doing it all day."

"Doing what?" Eva retorted.

"Smiling and singing – all that stuff you do when you've got a secret. Now I know what it is."

"So are you going to tell us?" Joel asked, carefully watching Eva's face, which was half-embarrassed, half-stubborn.

She shook her head and picked Holly up. "Let Karl read it out, since he thinks he's so clever."

So Karl began to read. "'Dear Tina' – it's an email," he explained. "'I know how much you love horses and ponies because you said it on your show on Saturday.'"

"Tina who?" Joel interrupted.

"Tina O'Neill, the chat show host," Karl explained. "Listen to the rest. 'My name is Eva Harrison and I live at an animal rescue centre called Animal Magic. Our motto is, "Matching the perfect pet with the perfect owner". Well, we've got a pony called Rosie who needs a new home.'" Karl paused for breath.

"I don't understand," Jen muttered.

"She's had one of her brilliant ideas," Karl cut in. "Listen. 'So I'd like you to have Rosie on your show so that lots of people can see her. Please say yes and help one poor pony find a brilliant new home. Thank you. From, Eva.'"

As Karl finished reading, Jen stood in astonished silence.

Eva frowned and held Holly tight, ready to be teased again. OK, so perhaps she'd been a bit hasty. Maybe she should have talked to the others first before she'd emailed Tina. Probably the big TV star was way too busy to take any notice...

"Magnificent!" Joel declared, beaming at her. "That's a totally brilliant idea, Eva. And I hope it works!"

Chapter Six

Tuesday and Wednesday passed in another flurry of dog walks and animal admissions ... and no reply from the famous chat show host.

At teatime a sad Annie came to visit Rosie.

"How's your mum?" Karl asked as he wheeled a barrow out of the stable.

"She's OK, but she's bored," Annie reported. "She can't do anything with her leg in plaster. How's Rosie?"

"Come and see," Eva said from inside the stable.

So Annie took a deep breath and reminded herself not to mope. She put on a smile and stroked Rosie, gave her a carrot and told her she was pleased to see her. "How's your poor leg?" she murmured.

"Much better," Eva told her. "Joel says that it'll be good as new in a day or two."

Rosie crunched the carrot contentedly, then nuzzled Annie's hand for more.

"All gone," Annie said with a smile. "You're so cheeky, Rosie!"

"Annie, I've got something to show you," Eva confided, pulling a crumpled copy of the email to Tina O'Neill out of her pocket. "Read this."

"Oh!" Annie gasped after she'd read it.

"We haven't had a reply yet, but what do you think?" Eva hoped Annie would approve. And she was glad she'd let her in on the plan.

There was a long silence as Annie's eyes filled with tears. "It's a cool idea – totally cool!" she whispered, backing out of the stables and leaving the yard just as Joel came out of the surgery with a visitor.

The two men headed straight for the stables where Eva was busy spreading clean straw. "Eva, meet Simon Cooper," Joel said. "Simon's a friend from college."

Eva looked up from her task. "Hi. Have you come to see Rosie?" she asked with a hopeful smile.

The visitor nodded. He was tall, like Joel, but heavier, with short, jet-black hair. He was wearing a shabby wax jacket, jeans and sturdy lace-up boots. "But I don't want to adopt her," he added quickly.

"Oh." Eva's face fell. She felt she was on a roller coaster of emotions – up, then down, up and down again.

"No. I've asked Simon to examine Rosie," Joel explained. "He's a horse osteopath and I want him to take a look at her back. Can you put her in a head collar and hold her steady while he looks her over?"

As Eva fastened the head collar, Simon gave the pony a quick stroke, then rolled up his sleeves. He began to lay his hands along Rosie's spine, pressing gently and watching her reactions.

"Is there something wrong?" Eva asked Joel anxiously. She didn't even know what the long word Joel had used meant.

"We're not sure yet. But you know Rosie's been acting oddly lately? Well, it occurred to me that there might be some hidden problem, and I noticed the other day she didn't like me touching her back. That's when I thought of asking Simon to have a look. As an osteopath, he knows all about bones and back problems."

Eva nodded tensely. She held Rosie's head collar while Simon examined her. The pony had all her attention on the visitor, with her ears flicked back and every nerve alert. Suddenly, as the osteopath's fingers hit a tender spot, she winced and pulled away.

"Steady!" Eva whispered, holding her firmly.

Simon concentrated on the problem spot, deep in the curve of her spine. "Ah!" he said. "This explains everything."

"So Simon massaged Rosie's spine!" Eva told her mum on the phone. "He sort of kneaded it until everything clicked back into place!"

"Magic!" Heidi said. "And this explains why Rosie wanted to get out of her stable – why she was kicking at the door?"

"Yes. Her back was hurting, so she needed to get out and run, and jump whatever got in her way – Simon says that's what horses do when they're in pain."

"And is she OK now?"

"She will be after another treatment."

"That's good news. And all thanks to Joel."

"Yes," Eva agreed. "We've found out what was wrong with Rosie and now all we have to do is get Tina O'Neill to find her a home!"

Chapter Seven

At nine o'clock that evening, Jen told Eva that it was time to shut down the computer. "Tina isn't going to reply to your email at this time of night," she insisted. "She's probably already in bed, getting her beauty sleep, which is what you have to do too."

"OK," Eva grunted as she reluctantly logged off.

"Never mind, it was worth trying." Even Karl had started being nice to her over her so-called crazy idea. "If it had worked out, it would have been cool to have Rosie on TV."

Eva sighed. "There must be something else we can do."

"Yes – get to bed!" Jen smiled as the phone began to ring. "Lay your head on that nice soft pillow and snooze."

"I will," Eva agreed, pausing to pick up the phone as she headed for the stairs.

"Hello. May I speak to Eva Harrison?" a woman's voice asked.

"That's me," Eva stammered. She stared wide-eyed at Karl and Jen.

"Eva, this is Francesca Wood. I'm sorry to call so late; I'm a researcher on the Tina O'Neill Show."

Eva almost dropped the phone. What should she say? What should she do?

"Hello?" the voice said. "Eva, are you still there?"

"Yes. It's me. I'm here."

"We got your recent email about the pony. I talked to Tina about it and we think your idea sounds interesting."

"Cool!" Eva gasped, as Karl and Jen moved closer to the phone and Holly ran between everyone's legs.

"So I looked Rosie up on your website and now I just want to check a few things with you," Francesca Wood said. "I need to ask you a few practical questions – is that OK?"

"Fine," Eva stammered.

"First, does the adult in charge of your rescue centre know that you sent us the email?"

Eva nodded, then realized Francesca couldn't see her. "I mean, yes. Jen's here right now."

"Good. I'll speak to her later. Second, has anyone else come forward to offer Rosie a home?"

"No. We haven't had a single enquiry."

"Excellent. Third, is Animal Magic down a narrow lane where our film crew would have difficulty with their large vans?"

"No. We're on Main Street in Okeham." Eva grew breathless as she tried to answer the quick-fire questions.

"And lastly, Tina wants us to be sure that there's nothing wrong with Rosie before we commit ourselves to giving her a slot on the Saturday show."

"How do you mean?" The question flustered Eva, then she remembered what Jen had said about not misleading people. She had to tell the truth. "Well, actually, Rosie did have a problem at her previous owners."

"Oh." Francesca's voice fell flat. "I'm sorry, Eva – that might put a stop to our featuring her on the show as we'd hoped."

"No, wait!" Eva cried. "The problem was to do with Rosie kicking her stable door and trying to run away, but we've just found out why she did it."

Standing close by, Jen was beginning to shake her head. Karl, too, looked disappointed.

"Rosie hurt her back," Eva explained to Tina O'Neill's researcher. "The horse osti – ostepa..."

"Oste-o-path!" Karl hissed.

"The horse osteopath came and fixed her. Now she's OK!" Gripping the phone and holding her breath, Eva waited for Francesca to speak again.

"Hmm. You're sure about this?"

"Totally! Rosie's cured. She's not a problem any more."

There was another pause, then Francesca made up her mind. "That sounds like a great story, Eva. And Rosie certainly looks cute in her photo. I think this is something we could do after all."

"Really?" Eva gasped.

"Yes, really," Francesca confirmed, her voice relaxing at last. "We'd definitely like to give Rosie a slot on our Saturday morning show."

"Tina O'Neill said yes!" Early next morning Eva rushed next door to Annie's house. She blurted out her conversation with Francesca Wood, then cycled up to her grandfather's garden centre. "Grandad, Rosie's going to be on the Tina O'Neill Show!"

Meanwhile, Karl dashed off to tell his friend George Stevens on Earlswood Avenue, and Miss Eliot at Swallow Court.

By nine o'clock, word had spread round the whole of Okeham.

Eva was cycling back to Animal Magic as a car marked with a film company's name drove up Main Street. "This way!" she yelled, standing at the gate.

Two men jumped out of the car, followed by a small, fair-haired woman. "Hi – Eva?" she asked. "I'm Francesca. Pleased to meet you."

As the men started to take a look around the yard, Karl showed up too. He and Eva proudly showed Francesca Wood around the centre.

"We've been open for less than two years," Karl explained. "Dad built the stables last year. This is where we keep Rosie."

"I think Simon's in here with Joel," Eva announced as she opened the door and led the visitor in. "Simon's the horse osteopath."

"Hi, Eva. I've finished Rosie's second treatment." Simon stroked the little pony's nose, then introduced himself to Francesca. "Joel has told me all about the slot on Tina's show. You can take it from me that this little pony won't have any more back problems. She's fit to go to a nice new home."

Rosie raised her head and neighed as if she was agreeing with him.

Francesca smiled. "Now then, Rosie, you have to be on your best behaviour tomorrow morning when Tina gets here."

"She will," Eva promised. Then she gave a nervous cough. "Erm, what's Tina like?" she asked, thinking of the sleek, glamorous woman in bright, tailored suits who appeared on the TV screen.

"Scary!" Francesca joked. "No, actually she's really nice and friendly. So don't be nervous. Perhaps you'd like to prepare a speech about Rosie – her history, what's happened to her lately, what kind of home you're looking for."

"A speech?" Eva stammered.

"Yes. Something nice and short. You'll be facing the camera with Rosie standing beside you. Our technical guys will set up lights and microphones here in the stable.

After your introduction to Rosie, Tina will ask you a few questions."

"Questions?" Eva gasped. She was beginning to quake in her shoes.

"Yes, just a friendly chat," Francesca assured her. She stood to one side as one of the crew came in to check the lighting. "OK, that's all for now," she told Eva. "I'll give you a call if there's anything else I need to know."

Chapter Eight

At seven o'clock on Friday morning, Eva laid out her horse combs and brushes, her shampoo, sprays, buckets and hoof oil. "Rosie, this is your big day," she said.

Outside it was dark, damp and cold – the start of a typical January day. Inside the stables the electric light cast a yellow glow.

Rosie sniffed the bucket filled with warm water and lavender shampoo, sighing as Eva gently sponged her back and withers.

"I've got a special detangler for your

mane to make it silky smooth," Eva told her. "You're going to smell gorgeous and look so-oo beautiful for the camera!"

It was hard work to groom Rosie to the point where she shone and sparkled, but at last Eva stood back to admire her. Looking at her watch, she saw it was a quarter to nine.

"Ready?" Karl asked, poking his head around the door. "The director and the camera and sound guys are already here. They're in the kitchen having coffee with Jen and Joel."

"Is Tina here yet?" Eva asked. She realized she had less than fifteen minutes to get changed and spruced up.

"She's on her way with Francesca." Karl stared at Eva's splashed sweatshirt and bedraggled hair. "Better get a move on," he warned.

Eva was in her bedroom, dressed in fresh jeans and her favourite red sweatshirt, drying her hair when she looked out of the window and saw a silver car pull into the yard.

She watched as a tall, slim woman with neatly cut blonde hair stepped out of the car into the chilly air. She was wearing a big blue scarf and a trendy dark blue jacket with silver zips.

"Eva, Tina's here!" Karl called from the foot of the stairs.

So she dashed down, rehearsing her speech word for word and trembling from top to toe.

Rosie is a five-year-old Shetland pony... She's fully schooled and loves children... We're looking for a home with other ponies...

"Hello – you must be Eva," Tina said, as Eva caught up with her and Francesca.

Eva felt her face turn red. Tina O'Neill was everything a TV star should be – glossy and smiley, with perfect hair and make-up. She mumbled hello and shuffled along, panicking in case she forgot her speech and let Rosie down.

"Everything's set up," Francesca told Tina as she guided her towards the stables.

"You did a good job in your email." Tina smiled at Eva. "I wish I'd been as smart when I was your age."

"Thanks," Eva muttered.

Tina went on chatting inside the stables as a make-up girl fussed and a sound man did a check. "So you love animals?" she asked Eva.

Eva nodded. *Rosie is a five-year-old Shetland pony... She's fully schooled...*

"Now tell us, Eva, what's special about Rosie?" Tina asked with a warm, encouraging smile.

It happened so fast that Eva didn't even know the camera was pointing at her.

"Rosie's clever," she answered. "She knows exactly what you're saying, especially if you're talking about her."

At that second, Rosie appeared at her stall door. She pushed it open and poked her head between Eva and their famous guest.

"See, she knows!" Eva smiled. "She can be quite cheeky, but she's never really naughty. And she loves being made a fuss of."

"And how come Rosie needs a new home?" Tina asked.

"Oh, that's because she had a problem," Eva explained in a rush.

"A problem pony?" Tina interrupted. "I guess that makes it especially hard to rehome her?"

"It could do, but we hope not. When she lived at her last place, she used to kick the stable door and try to run away." Suddenly, Eva noticed that the camera light was on and pointing in her direction. *Oh no!* she thought. *I've ruined it for Rosie. Now no one will want her.* And she stopped dead.

Tina O'Neill carried on smiling at the camera. "But luckily that's not the end of Rosie's story," she told the viewers. "Here we are with a lovely little Shetland who had a couple of behavioural problems that seemed to rule her out for adoption. But, Eva, tell everyone what happened next."

Eva pulled herself together. *Don't be nervous,* she told herself, *concentrate on Rosie and do your best for her.* "We found out what was wrong soon after she came back here," she explained. "It turned out Rosie had a bad back – the horse osteopath said it was a trapped nerve which was hurting and making her act up."

"Really?" Tina interrupted. "That's interesting. What looked like naughtiness turned out to be a physical problem after all."

That was it exactly! Eva nodded eagerly. "Simon cured it and now Rosie's a perfect pony again!"

"That's wonderful, Eva – it really is." As Rosie nudged the glamorous visitor with her nose, Tina rounded off the interview. "We're looking for a real fairy-tale ending," she explained to the camera. "Animal Magic is a fabulous rescue centre set up to match the perfect pet with the perfect owner. When Eva emailed us an emergency appeal for help, we decided it was time for the Tina O'Neill show to step in."

Rosie snuggled up to Tina and seemed to nod. Her bright eyes sparkled and her shiny mane shone like silk.

Tina's smile broadened. "So if anyone watching already has a pony who needs a friend and stable mate, we'd like you to contact Animal Magic directly. Details are on your screen right now."

Chapter Nine

At nine o'clock next morning Eva, Karl, Jen and Joel were glued to the TV screen.

"Tina said we get the first slot on the Saturday show," Karl reminded them.

"I can't bear to look!" Eva sighed, hugging Holly and hoping that she didn't come across as a total idiot.

"Ten – nine – eight – seven..." Joel counted down as the Tina O'Neill signature tune began.

"Good morning, Britain!" Tina greeted

her viewers warmly from the studio. "Today we're starting with a feel-good story about Rosie the problem pony who turns out not to be such a problem after all!"

Karl nudged Eva and grinned at her. Jen turned up the volume and listened intently.

"Yesterday I spent the day at a wonderful rescue centre called Animal Magic," Tina went on as the scene changed to their own yard.

"It's us – we're on!" Karl cried. "Look, there's our house!"

"And the kennels and the cattery!" Eva watched as the camera panned round towards the stables. "We're actually on TV – wow!"

"Animal Magic is a very special place – and I'm here to meet a wonderful new friend," Tina explained, well wrapped up in her blue scarf and jacket.

The camera swung away from her and captured Eva leading the way into the stables.

"It's you!" Karl yelled.

"Sshh! I know it's me." Eva got ready to cringe with embarrassment.

"And Rosie," Jen added, as for the first time the little pony stuck her head over her stall door and posed for the camera.

"Meet Rosie," Tina said, "and her carer, Eva Harrison. Now tell us, Eva, what's so special about Rosie?"

"Rosie's clever," Eva explained to her guest. Her red sweatshirt made her look bright and cheerful. Her long hair was neatly tied back, with only a wisp or two escaping from her ponytail. "She knows exactly what you're saying, especially if you're talking about her..."

"Amazing!" Joel grinned as Tina ended the slot and took the viewers back to the Saturday morning studio. "You're a TV natural," he told Eva.

"That was cool," Karl agreed. "I'd

definitely want to adopt Rosie after watching that."

Eva sighed happily. "How cute did Rosie look!"

"And now we all have to get over to Reception in double quick time," Joel told them. "With luck, viewers will be ringing us already."

So they turned off the TV and hurried across the yard to find the Animal Magic phone red hot with callers.

"I'm interested in your Shetland pony," one viewer of Tina's show explained to Jen. "Can you tell me again how old Rosie is?"

Or, "Rosie is the ideal pony for my six-year-old daughter. She looks such fun!"

Or, "I fell in love with the pony on the Tina O'Neill Show. Can I drive over with my mum to see her?"

For a full hour the phone didn't stop ringing.

"We have to write down names and phone numbers." From the start Jen was the organized one. "Karl, here's the diary. Can you make a note of times when people want to come?"

"How old is your daughter?" Joel asked one eager caller. "No, I'm afraid three's a bit too young. Wait a year or two then have another look at our website. We'll always have ponies who need new homes. Thank you for calling. Goodbye."

"How many people definitely want to come and see Rosie?" Eva asked Karl after another hour had passed.

Together they checked the diary and counted eight definite appointments.

"The first people say they can get here by eleven this morning," Karl said.

"Hello, I see you're run off your feet, as expected." Jimmy Harrison arrived in Reception with a broad smile. "Where's my TV star granddaughter?"

Eva grinned back. "Was it OK?"

"Eva, I was so proud, I nearly burst!"

"Hi, Jimmy," Joel took a break between phone calls. "And hi, Annie. Did you see Eva on the telly?"

Annie had just arrived in the doorway. "You were great," she told Eva with a smile. "Have you had many phone calls?"

"Hundreds," Eva replied. "The TV idea worked really well."

"So Rosie won't be here much longer?" Annie seemed to hover uneasily by the door. "Mum's here with me. Do you mind if we go and see her one last time?"

"I'll come too." Quickly Eva left the desk and ran to join Annie and Linda. Linda looked pale and leaned heavily on crutches to cross the yard.

"This is the hard bit," Linda sighed as they went into the stables. "I know that we've done the right thing, but I'm still so fond of little Rosie."

"I know. I hate saying goodbye to our animals," Eva admitted. "I always wish they could stay."

"But we've still got Gwinnie and Merlin." Linda tried to look on the bright side.

"And you promise us you won't let Rosie go to just any old person," Annie pleaded, softly stroking Rosie's nose.

"I totally promise!" Eva replied. "She'll go to the best place because she deserves it, don't you, Rosie?"

The bright little Shetland gave a short neigh, then went back to munching hay from her net. *Don't bother me while I'm eating,* she seemed to say. *Come back later when I'm ready for visitors!*

An hour later, Eva was back in the stables for the first appointment. "Come and meet Emma and her mum," she told Rosie, leading her out into the yard.

"Aah!" Emma Bridges squealed the moment Rosie trotted into view. "She's beautiful. I want her, Mum – please, please, please!"

Rosie snorted and tossed her head.

I agree, Eva thought. *Emma's voice is too screechy, and she shouldn't stamp her feet like that.*

Next on the appointment list came Jake

Wade with his father, Julian. Jake was quiet and calm and Rosie seemed to like him. But he was too tall to ride her and so his dad said no thank you.

Then there was nervous Carla Simpson with her big sister, Zara. Carla burst into tears when Rosie nudged her pocket, asking for a treat.

Then came twin girls, Amy and Lucy, who wanted to share Rosie and argued straight away over who would have the first ride.

By midday, Eva had trotted Rosie out into the yard half a dozen times without success.

"Maybe the TV thing wasn't such a good idea after all," she sighed.

Fed-up little Rosie seemed to agree, searching Eva's pocket for a carrot.

But then Karl brought over a couple called Mr and Mrs Baker and their daughter, Martha. "They live in the next dale, twenty miles away," he said.

"Sorry we couldn't get here earlier," Mrs Baker told Eva. "We had an appointment with our farrier. He came to shoe my husband's horse, Dexter, and it was too late to change his time."

"What do you think of Rosie?" Mr Baker asked Martha. "Do you like her?"

"She's pretty," Martha said. "She looks a bit like Daisy."

"Daisy was Martha's last pony," her mother explained. "Sadly, Daisy was very old and died last autumn. We've been looking around for another Shetland ever since."

All this time Rosie had stood quietly beside Eva, but now she took a step forward and began to nudge Martha's arm in a let-me-be-your-friend way.

"And friendly." Martha smiled. "Look, Dad – she likes me!"

"I think she does," Mr Baker agreed. "And we all like *her*, don't we?"

Eva stood well back, letting Rosie do her stuff. *So-oo smart!* she thought.

"So shall we give her a home?" Mrs Baker asked. "Shall we put her in the stable next to Dexter and let you two ride out together? What do you say?"

Martha put her arm around Rosie's neck. "Yes, please!" she sighed.

And Rosie nodded so that her mane fell forward and she peeked at Eva with a mischievous gleam in her eye.

Chapter Ten

"So this is Rosie's last day in Okeham?" Mark led Heidi, Karl and Eva across the yard to the stables.

It was Tuesday, and Mark and Heidi were back from their holiday looking tanned and relaxed. Their bulging suitcases were still in the car. Inside the house, Joel was saying goodbye to Jen, ready to head back to Russia.

"It's Rosie's very last *morning*," Eva said. "The Bakers are bringing their horsebox this afternoon and driving Rosie to their place."

"Which we went and checked out with Jen," Karl explained. "They live in a massive house with loads of stables and a big paddock. It's like a luxury hotel for horses!"

"And they're really nice people." Now that the day had come, Eva was more excited than sad. "Martha loves ponies!"

"As much as you?" her dad asked with a smile. He held the stable door open while Eva, Karl and Heidi went in.

"*No one* loves ponies as much as Eva!" Karl cried. "That would be impossible."

"Hey, you hear that, Rosie?" Eva sighed, putting her arm around the pony's neck. "They're making fun of me and saying I'm crazy about you!"

Rosie nudged Eva's cheek with her nose.

"Well, you definitely did a good job of rehoming this little girl," Heidi told Eva. "I don't think anyone could have tried harder or had a better idea than getting her on the Tina O'Neill Show!"

Eva beamed at her mum and dad. "Even Annie and Linda are happy in the end. The Bakers are happy. Rosie's happy. *I'm* happy!"

"And it made wonderful publicity for Animal Magic," Heidi added, smiling at Eva.

"Which can't be bad," her dad added. He looked round the stables at three smiling faces. "I'm glad to be back," he told them all. "Florida was great, but there's honestly and truly no better place to come back to than Animal Magic Rescue Centre!"

Collect all the books
in the series!